Bright **≡Summaries**.com

The Cloven Viscount

BY ITALO CALVINO

BOOK ANALYSIS

Written by Marion Munier
Translated by Oliver Brown

The Cloven Viscount

BY ITALO CALVINO

ITALO CALVINO

- **Born in 1923 in Santiago de Las Vegas (Cuba)**
- **Died in 1985 in Siena (Italy)**
- **Some of his works:**
  - *The Spider's Nest Trail* (1947), novel
  - *Marcovaldo or Seasons in the City* (1958 and 1963), novel
  - *The Castle of Crossed Destinies* (1973), short stories

Italo Calvino was two years old when his family left Cuba for Italy, his parents' country of origin. There he received an anti-fascist education. During the Second World War (1939-1945), he fought in the Italian resistance, an experience that nourished his first novel, *The Path of the Spiders' Nests*. While pursuing a career as a journalist, he continued to write.

He gained public recognition in the 1950s with the publication of his trilogy of stories, *Nos ancêtres*. In 1960, he moved to Paris and, at the request of Raymond Queneau (French writer, 1903-1976), joined OuLiPo (OUvroir de LIttérature POtentielle) in 1974, which brought together experimental authors. He continued to publish numerous works, including *Les Villes invisibles* in 1972. His imagination, lucidity and humour make him an author for young and old alike, and one of the freest writers of his time.

THE CLOVEN VISCOUNT

AN ALLEGORICAL VISION OF THE HUMAN CONDITION

- **Genre:** Storytelling

- **Reference edition:** *Le Vicomte pourfendu*, translated from Italian by Juliette Bertrand, Paris, Albin Michel, « Le Livre de Poche » series, 1955, 123 p.

- **1st edition:** 1952

- **Themes :** duality, goodness, cruelty, humour, fantasy, wonder, war

Le Vicomte pourfendu is the first book in the trilogy *Nos ancêtres*, which also includes *Le Baron perché* (1957) and *Le Chevalier inexistant* (1959). These three fables offer an allegorical vision of the human condition.

Le Vicomte pourfendu (*The Cloven Viscount*) tells the story of the life of Viscount Médard, who was cut in two vertically by a cannonball. Since then, each part of his body has lived independently; the right one is evil and brings misfortune to his village, while the left one is good and only does good. In so doing, Italo Calvino illustrates the complexity of the human being, and shows that goodness and cruelty, when taken to extremes, are equally inhuman.

SUMMARY

THE WRONG HALF

Viscount Médard of Terralba goes to war against the Turks with his squire, Kurt. Although Kurt explains the disasters of the battlefield to him, Lieutenant Médard is eager to fight. But in a violent battle, Kurt is wounded, while the Viscount is hit by a cannonball that cuts him in half vertically.

When he returns, the villagers discover that he has lost the left side of his body. Something has changed in him, and the Viscount refuses to visit his father, the old Aiulphe, who sends him his favourite bird to make contact: Médard tortures the animal and cuts it in two. The next day, the patriarch is found dead in his aviary.

The villagers soon discover that the Viscount cuts everything in half: fruit, plants and animals. He even gives his nephew (his sister's son born out of wedlock) halves of poisonous mushrooms to fricassee, which makes his old nurse, Sébastienne, say that "it's Médard's bad half that's come back" (p. 29). Subsequently, this part of the Viscount does not stop trying to kill his nephew.

The Viscount, who is presiding over a trial against brigands, has become tyrannical and decides that the accused, as well as the victims, should be hanged.

Moreover, pretending to want to help Dr Trelawney, who has abandoned medicine to take an interest in insects and ammonites, Médard has some peasants executed: in this way, he will be able to fill the cemetery and thus provoke the will-o'-the-wisps that the scientist is studying.

The Viscount now has a fire fetish and sets fires everywhere, sometimes killing peasants. He even sets fire to part of his own castle: his nurse is injured, but he claims that her burns were symptoms of leprosy. Unable to bear her criticism, he decides to get rid of the old woman and sends her to Préchampignon, the place where leprosy patients spend their time playing musical instruments.

Médard's nephew, disappointed with Dr Trelawney – who refused to examine Sébastienne – decides to approach a family of Huguenots (Calvinist Protestants) from France and becomes friends with Esau, a young man fascinated by sin. The Huguenots keep a close eye on their house to preserve it from the Viscount's incendiary madness.

One day, during a violent storm, he comes to ask for their hospitality; he tries to bribe them and lure them to the castle, but the Huguenots refuse. Vexed, Médard leaves, threatening them. When Médard's nephew goes to Préchampignon to find Sébastienne, he discovers that the lepers are indulging in orgies; the nurse takes him away and gives him a cure for the disease.

THE GOOD AND THE UNFORTUNATE REUNITED

As Viscount Médard considers that being half of himself allows him to understand and feel things better (p. 60), he decides to fall in love, sure that at home "this passion will certainly be magnificent and terrible" (p. 61).

He sets his sights on Pamela, a little shepherdess, to whom he gives an appointment. She goes, but refuses to follow him to the castle, where he wants to lock her up. Médard threatens her parents, who give in and are ready to hand over their daughter. To escape from the Viscount, Pamela decides to hide in a cave in the forest with a duck and a goat.

The next day, the Viscount saves his nephew from drowning and, in order to protect him, is bitten instead by a poisonous spider. The young man is surprised that Médard is not dressed as usual and that he is being kind. In search of an herb to cure the bite, he goes to Sébastienne's house, but when he meets his uncle again, he is dealing with the wrong half. Distraught, the young man tells his adventures to Dr Trelawney, who seems to think it is not the same Viscount, but says no more. Médard's duality is later confirmed: he alternates between good and bad actions via his two halves.

When Pamela meets the Viscount, she too understands that he has a dual personality: "The Viscount who lives in the castle, the evil one, is one half. You are the other half, who was thought to have disappeared in the war and who has returned." (p. 87). Médard's good half tells how two hermits found him on the battlefield and healed him. When Pamela reveals to him that his bad half is pursuing her and terrifying the whole region with her barbarity, the Viscount's good half confesses his love for her.

Each time he visits the patients, the doctor – accompanied by Médard's nephew – notices that the good Viscount has preceded him there; he sees the mark left by the latter outside the house, informing him of the patient's problem. But his evil half, nicknamed the Unfortunate, never fails to appear and sow evil. The Good One continues to do good, however, a task in which Pamela assists him, while the Unfortunate One tries, in vain, to kill him.

The Good Man asks the carpenter Pierreclou to create devices that are activated by goodness and not by evil, but he comes up empty. His henchmen then suggest that Le Bon attack the Unfortunate in his place, but he refuses. In the meantime, the carpenter builds a gallows "to be hung in profile" (p. 105), which the Unfortunate One has ordered for him.

Only the old Sébastienne does not appreciate the Good: she blames him for the bad actions of his other half. Moreover, according to her, in wanting to do good, he sometimes causes evil. For example, he constantly lectures lepers who, finding no comfort, are deprived of music and debauchery because of him, sink into despair. Other people gradually come around to the nurse's opinion and begin to criticise the Good, believing that "of the two halves the good is worse than the bad" (p. 110).

In the meantime, both sides of the Viscount ask her parents for Pamela's hand in marriage: the Good wants to sacrifice himself so that she will marry the Unfortunate, the Unfortunate that she will marry the Good – so that he can then claim her as his lawful wife. The young woman decides to marry the Good, but the Unfortunate then asserts his rights.

The two halves of Médard argue and fight in a duel, during which their scars open up. However, Dr Trelawney manages to sew the two halves together and heal them. Médard becomes the same person he was before the war: neither good nor bad. After that, the doctor sails back to Captain Cook's ship, leaving the nephew of the Viscount alone.

CHARACTER STUDIES

VISCOUNT MEDARD OF TERRALBA

The Young Medard

No physical description of Viscount Medard is given; we only know that he is young when he goes to war. His innocence blinds him, and he is eager to fight while surrounded by death, suffering and consternation. His fearlessness makes him ignore danger until he is cut in half by a cannon shot.

The Unfortunate and the Good

The Unfortunate One – the right half – tortures animals and human beings. He is cruel and likes to make people suffer. According to him, "beauty, wisdom and justice exist only in what is torn to pieces" (p. 60). His savagery is gratuitous, but he seems to be sensitive to a certain aesthetics of suffering, hence the construction of gallows that force everyone to admire their beauty and ingenuity.

His attempt to make the Huguenots his allies, by converting to their faith, is only an opportunity to consider a war against the Catholic princes. But the integrity of the Protestants is stronger than him and his threat to denounce their presence to the Inquisition. The Unfortunate One leaves their house, furious. Lightning strikes nearby, no doubt sent by the devil, for the tree hit is half charred from head to foot.

The good man – the left half – seems to want only to do good, but the villagers soon discover the ambiguity of this approach. Indeed, he often provokes evil by dint of his virtue. For example, he turns the lepers away from their pleasures (music and debauchery), which leads to their despair.

The Reassembled Viscount

Once restored, the Viscount "became a whole man again, neither wicked nor good, mixed with goodness and wickedness, that is to say, a being not differing in appearance from what he had been before he was struck down" (p. 121). He then lives happily with Pamela and has many children.

In *The Cloven Viscount*, Médard's dissociation refers to *The Strange Case of Dr.. Jekyll and Mr. Hyde* (1886) by Robert Louis Stevenson (Scottish writer, 1850-1894). But the comparison stops at the theme of duality, because the metamorphosis of Jekyll (the good guy) into Hyde (the criminal) finally gives the latter supremacy in a fantasy story, with the added horror.

THE NARRATOR

The name of the narrator is unknown. We know that he is the nephew of the Viscount, the son – born out of wedlock – of his sister and a poacher. Orphaned, he seems to have been taken in as a child by his grandfather and brought up by the nurse Sébastienne. He lives in a hut in the forest and grows fond of Dr Trelawney, then of the Huguenots and finally of Pamela, the shepherdess. After the doctor leaves, he is left alone and sad. He is 7 or 8 years old at the beginning of the story, and reaches adolescence at the end.

His willingness to tell stories is frustrated when the situation in the lordship returns to normal. So he retires to the woods and imagines stories just for himself; it is his way of sublimating reality.

DR TRELAWNEY

Dr Trelawney travelled the oceans on Captain James Cook's ship (British navigator, 1728-1779). The character's name is taken from an adventure novel, *Treasure Island* (1883) by R. L. Stevenson.

At the beginning of the story, he does not heal anyone, but is rather interested in plants, stones and will-o'-the-wisps. Gradually he returns to medicine and takes an interest in the Viscount's case, which he finally succeeds in putting back together by reassembling the two halves. At the end of the story he sets sail again.

PAMELA

Pamela is a young shepherdess who can communicate with animals. Both parts of the Viscount fall in love with her. Brave and determined, she resists the assaults of the Unfortunate One, but seems to have a fondness for the Good One.

Disappointed by her parents, who want to abandon her to the Unfortunate One, she leaves to live in the forest. Nevertheless, at the end of the tale, she ends up marrying the Viscount. She rejoices at his reassembly and exclaims, "I will finally have a husband with all his attributes." (p. 121).

Of low extraction, without protection – not even that of her parents who have opted for obedience to the Viscount's wishes – the young girl knows how to defend her virtue and resist the one everyone fears, even if it means choosing to live in the forest until things calm down.

Cleverly, she does not pass up this proposal of marriage that would change her life. So she goes to each of the halves, since there are halves, to give her consent. One could say that she instinctively knows what she has to do; her approach will provoke the duel (the Good against the Unfortunate) from which a complete husband will emerge!

In other words, in *Le Vicomte pourfendu*, the woman – or love – reconciles the parties. Like the creature depicted by Samuel Richardson (English writer, 1689-1761) in *Pamela or Virtue Rewarded* (1740), Italo Calvino's Pamela achieves a successful social rise.

SÉBASTIENNE

Sébastienne is the old nurse who raised the Viscount. She is above all the only one who opposes him. He sends her to live with the lepers after he tries to kill her in a fire. She condemns both parts of the Viscount, because for her, neither one corresponds to the child – and later to the young man – whom she took care of before the war and whom she considers her son. She is the first to warn the others: "It's the wrong half of Médard that has come back." (p. 29).

As a witness to what he has been and will no longer be, Sébastienne becomes an unbearable presence for Médard, and one who, moreover, reproaches him: "[Leprosy] is nothing, my son, compared to the evil that awaits you in hell if you do not repent." (p. 45). This is why he wants this emotional figure to disappear.

MASTER PIERRECLOU

Master Pierreclou, saddler and carpenter, lacks courage and is unhappy about it. He puts his art at the service of evil, even though he would like to apply his passion for mechanisms to building machines dedicated to something other than hanging people. Instead of opposing the Unfortunate One's orders, he redoubles his ingenuity in his systems to marvel at them himself and thus manages to conceal their use. A fine example of not resisting tyranny – or coming to terms with it – which contrasts with that of Sébastienne.

KEYS TO READING

A FANTASTIC OR WONDERFUL STORY?

Tzvetan Todorov (literary theorist, French literary critic of Bulgarian origin, 1939-2017) defines the fantastic as "the hesitation experienced by a being who knows only the natural laws in the face of an apparently supernatural event" (TODOROV T, *Introduction à la littérature fantastique*, Paris, Seuil, 1970, p. 51). In other words, inexplicable elements occur, and it is difficult to assess whether they are real or supernatural: are they a pure illusion of the senses, a creation of the imagination in an ordinary universe, or do they really take place in a world that therefore transgresses the natural laws as we know them?

Italo Calvino's *The Cloven Viscount does* not, at first sight, seem to meet Todorov's criteria. In fact, through his speech, the narrator leaves no doubt as to the reality of events. From the very first chapter and throughout the story, the supernatural elements that appear seem completely normal to the characters. For example, storks devour corpses ("'[They] feed on human flesh,' replied the squire, 'now that famine has made the countryside arid and drought has dried up the rivers'", p. 6), and the courtesans are infested with scorpions and lizards, which is hardly surprising.

Similarly, while the arrival of the Viscount in the village terrifies the inhabitants, they seem to take his condition – he is reduced to half of himself – for granted and do not question the reasons for his survival. They all accept that a being cut in two can live; later, his reassembly seems no more complicated than that. The narrator explains: "The doctor had been careful to match all the viscera and arteries on both sides." (p. 120). The operation, which takes barely half an hour, restores the Viscount's physical integrity and, again, no one is surprised.

This accumulation of unreal facts accepted by the characters in the tale thus makes the story swing towards the marvellous genre. In contrast to the fantastic, the latter is characterised by the irruption of supernatural facts that are accepted within the world represented – this is the world of magic and enchantment.

However, if we take into account the fact that the narrator is only about ten years old, this could explain the supernatural tinge of this story and the impression of naivety that emerges. In fact, from the very first lines of *Le Vicomte pourfendu*, we learn that the narrator is in fact the nephew of the main character of the story, narrated in the first person singular: "We were at war with the Turks. Viscount Medard de Terralba, my uncle, was riding across the plains of Bohemia." (p. 5).

Although the first two chapters recount events that took place on the battlefield, and the narrator accurately transcribes the conversations between the

Viscount and his squire, we discover at the beginning of the third chapter that he was not present. He says: "I was seven or eight years old when my uncle returned to Terralba." (p. 19).

Between the marvellous and the fantastic, the reader can then have doubts: does the unreality of the story not come from the imagination and naivety of the child who has transcribed with fantasy facts that are explicable for adults? Is the wonder really omnipresent or is the child distorting what he has experienced? At the end of the story, when everything is back to normal, does he not say, sadly and idly:

> *"[I] still hid in the woods between the roots of the tall trees to tell myself stories. A pine needle could represent a knight, a lady or a jester to me; I would wave it before my eyes, and endless stories would exhilarate me. Then I would blush at these musings and run away. (p. 122)*

He thus confesses his penchant for fabrication, and feels almost guilty about it. We could also see in this confession – the same procedure is used in *The Perched Baron* – a facetiousness of the author who is laughing at himself for having invented such an extraordinary story!

In the end, it is therefore difficult to define the status of the text, which depends on the point of view adopted by the reader:

- either the latter accepts all the elements as plausible, and the text is a marvel;
- or he doubts the veracity of the story and finds an explanation in the narrator's youth: the reading experience is then fantastic.

A PHILOSOPHICAL TALE

The Question of Good and Evil

From the very first lines, the protagonists, Viscount Medard and his squire Kurt, are reminiscent of (and pastiche with) another literary couple from 17th century Spain, the knight Don Quixote and his faithful Sancho Panza (*The Ingenious Hidalgo Don Quixote de la Mancha*, published in two parts, 1605 and 1615) by Miguel de Cervantes (Spanish novelist, poet and playwright, 1547-1616). The Viscount is enthusiastic about going to fight for the Christians against the Turks, and comically naive about the realities of war. Fortunately, his squire is there to answer all his questions:

> *"From time to time there is a finger pointing the way," asked my uncle Medard. What does that mean?*
>
> *– May God forgive them! The living cut off the fingers of the dead to take their rings. (p. 8)*

Then, very quickly, after the assault that cuts the Viscount in two, the story takes on a marvellous character, told from the point of view of the narrator, Médard's young nephew. This half of the man intrigues the reader; but when he understands that he is dealing with the incarnation of evil, the story becomes more disturbing. And when the other half, the incarnation of good, finally appears, the story takes a moral turn which gives it its didactic function and its philosophical dimension on the model of *Candide ou l'Optimisme* (1759) by Voltaire (writer and philosopher of the Enlightenment, 1694-1778), master of the philosophical tale, or of *Jacques le Fataliste et son maître* (1796) by Denis Diderot (encyclopaedist and philosopher of the Enlightenment, 1713-1784).

Evil on the one hand, and good on the other, both exercise a tyranny that is not suitable for the smooth running of the world. It is easy to understand how, as far as the evil is concerned, the good Medard's action is flawed by an excess of naivety, good feelings and morality practised without nuance:

- To the plan of the conspirators who want to "massacre" (p. 106) the tyrant, the good Médard substitutes that of offering him an ointment. As a result, "the viscount sentenced them to the gallows" (p. 107);

- To the lepers, he removes the licentious pleasures that made them forget their condition, causing them to affirm that "of the two halves, the good is worse than the bad" (p. 110);

- As for the Huguenots, dedicated to hard work, they do not understand his exhortation to give to the poorest. "Doing charity, my brother [says one of the Huguenots] does not mean losing out on prices." (p. 100).

And so the narrator concludes: "We felt as if we were lost between an equally inhuman virtue and perversity" (p. 110), whereas the human being is composed of both. In the happy ending, the final reunion of the two halves forms a whole man, and no doubt a better one after this experience. However, "it is not enough to have a complete viscount for the whole world to be complete"

(p. 122) because, Italo Calvino seems to suggest, perfection is not of this world...

The Duality of Being

Le Vicomte pourfendu (The Split Viscount) tells the story of how a man cut in two by a cannonball becomes a literal double: one part of his body embodies goodness, while the other represents evil. In so doing, the author depicts a world in which, when goodness or badness reigns supreme, life is impossible, because it is inhuman; above all, he begins a reflection on human nature, which is fundamentally dual.

It is interesting to note that even before he is wounded, the young man's character is already ambiguous. His relationship to war manifests this duality: he is happy to go to war and happy to have killed the first Turk – in this he can be considered evil – but in the context of the Ottoman wars in Europe (between the 14th and 18th centuries), killing a non-Catholic is still considered a salvific act.

The fact of war that mutilated the Viscount is answered by the duel that brings the two halves face to face on the day of the wedding with Pamela. If we refer to an early Latin etymology of "duel", *duellum,* an archaic form of "war", this confrontation can be read as a fight that unites (the two halves of the Viscount) and leads to a good, as opposed to the war that separates and destroys. If we refer rather to *dualis,* to the notion of "two", the duel can also be interpreted as the indispensable test through which the Viscount must pass in order to regain his integrity, a fight other than the one on the battlefield: a fight against himself in order to regain what he really is, a man with his good and bad sides.

AN INITIATION STORY

Towards the Fulfilment of the Hero

Different from the apprenticeship story, the initiation story implies the "intimate transformation of the personality, presented in a symbolic rather than realistic way, with the discovery of new values, often accompanied by suffering" (« Les récits initiatiques », in cndp.fr). In this vein, we can read, among others, novels such as *Vendredi ou la Vie sauvage* (1971) by Michel Tournier (French writer, 1924-2016) and *L'Île mystérieuse* (1874) by Jules Verne (French writer, 1828-1905).

Beyond good and evil, we can reflect on what Italo Calvino himself says about The *Cloven Viscount*, which can lead us to consider this tale as an initiatory story: for the author, it is indeed a question of staging an "aspiration to a completeness [of oneself] beyond the mutilations imposed by society" (quoted in FUSCO M., « Un arbre généalogique ? », in *Europe*, n° 815, March 1997, p. 32).

Thus Viscount Medard de Terralba, who at the beginning of the story is "in his early youth, an age when feelings have only a confused impulse in which good and evil are not yet distinct" (p. 6), becomes, at the end of his journey, this "whole man, neither wicked nor good, mixed with goodness and wickedness, that is to say, a being not differing, in appearance, from what he had been before he was slain. But he had experience of both halves together: so he must have been wise." (p. 121).

In fact, when he is only bad, his judgement is distorted, and he says to his nephew, for example: "And you too will want everything to be torn apart in your own image, because beauty, wisdom and justice exist only in that which is torn apart." (p. 60). When he is only good, he discovers the brotherhood that binds him to whole people, but he perceives them as incomplete beings.

Hence his compassion develops: "It is not I alone, Pamela, who am torn apart and torn to pieces, but you too, all of us." (p. 89). Once the distinction between good and evil is clearly established in his mind, the Viscount can return to a normal life, where intimate happiness is possible by starting a family.

The Storyteller's Apprenticeship

In *The Cloven Viscount*, this search for self is not foreign to the young nephew either. He is seven or eight years old at the beginning of the story, and a teenager at the end; he is the witness and reporter of the Viscount's initiatory experience, through which his own life is threatened several times (in the episode with the poisonous mushrooms [p. 29], in the episode with the footbridge [p. 36], and in the episode with the fishing [p. 60]). As the narrator, it is he who draws the moral of these episodes. Yet, at first sight, he does not seem to be able to blossom: "I, alone, in the midst of this fervour of integrity, felt more and more alone and lacking. Sometimes one believes oneself to be incomplete simply because one is young" (p. 122), he adds.

Is this a joke on the part of the author, who does not want to end on an optimistic note, because nothing is perfect? Or a desire to represent himself in this character who, once this story is over, has nothing more to say, even though his raison d'être is unfailingly to tell other stories? At the end of the day (of the tale), if the young man has made an apprenticeship, it is perhaps that of the storyteller: "I had reached the threshold of adolescence and was still hiding in the woods between the roots of the big trees to tell myself stories. [...] endless stories exhilarated me." (p. 122). This seems to be his role: all that remains is for him to assume it for other stories to come.

A HUMOROUS WORK

Italo Calvino "points out [...] that he began this book in 1951, that is to say, at a time when the euphoria of the end of the [Second World War] had already given way to the tensions, both internal and external, which were once again weighing down everywhere [the Cold War, 1945-1990]." (FUSCO M., «Un arbre généalogique?», p. 30). However, *Le Vicomte pourfendu* is a work in which humour plays a predominant role. The author uses different processes to paint a violent and cruel world in a distanced way:

- **The metaphor becomes real.** For example, the first soldier the Viscount and his squire meet on the battlefield complains of "taking root" (p. 9), even though he is covered in moss and mildew;

- **Hyperbole.** Characters and facts are described in excess. For example, the courtesans in the camp are swarming with beasts and "are no longer just covered with ticks, bugs and crabs; scorpions and green lizards make their nests on them." (*ibid.*) Similarly, the doctor uses no less than "a mile of tape" (p. 120) to assemble the two halves of the Viscount;

- **Irony.** The author depicts a world out of step with what it should be and plays with appearances. Thus, the Huguenot's son indulges in all sorts of sins, Sébastienne, the nurse, proves to be a better doctor than the doctor, who is petrified of the sick, and Master Pierreclou's gallows becomes a work of art that everyone comes to regret when it is removed;

- **Macabre humour.** On several occasions, the author diverts the macabre of the descriptions or facts with touches of humour. On the battlefield, for example, severed fingers point the characters in the right direction, and storks replace vultures in devouring the corpses.

Thus, *The Cloven Viscount* can be placed in the hands of a young audience who, in the manner of the nephew-narrator, will approach it from a marvellous point of view, will be entertained by the adventures encountered by the characters and will perhaps learn something moral from them.

Le Vicomte pourfendu has the ability to carry the reader at high speed from one situation to another, giving rise to a succession of impressions and feelings that entertain, amaze or frighten the reader. It is not possible to identify with the characters – the time and form of the tale do not lend themselves to this – but the reader will easily be able to identify the author's intention thanks to the clarity of the writing, to this fantasy and humour which serve, in a limpid manner, the moral and philosophical demonstration.

A FEW QUESTIONS FOR FURTHER REFLECTION…

- Considering her condition as a poor girl, Pamela, the shepherdess, shows an unexpected character that makes her a particularly positive character. Expand on this.

- The Unfortunate One justifies his evil deeds by saying that being maimed gives him a more complete view of reality. What do you think of this?

- Is it love or hate that allows the reconstruction of the Viscount? Justify your answer.

- In Chapter IX, some lepers say that "of the two halves, the good half is worse than the bad" (p. 110). What do you think about this? Support your answer with the text.

- How does the author view war in this work?

- In your opinion, is the author seeking a realistic effect or not? Justify this.

- In their book, *Le fantastique*, Gilbert Millet and Denis Labbé propose to define this genre as "the inconceivable become reality" (*Le fantastique*, Paris, Belin, coll. «Sujets», 2005, p. 11), which only works with the assent of the reader who accepts the implausible. Do you think this definition applies to The *Cloven Viscount*?

- Compare the character of Viscount Médard with that of Clarimonde in *La Morte amoureuse* (1836), a fantastic short story by Théophile Gauthier (French writer, 1811-1872).

- Italo Calvino refers to R. L. Stevenson's *Treasure Island* by reusing the name Trelawney. R. L. Stevenson also wrote *Doctor Jekyll and Mr. Hyde*. What similarities and dissimilarities can you find between this work and *The Cloven Viscount*?

- "Doctor! Doctor Trelawney! Take me with you! You can't leave me here, Doctor!" (p. 123), the nephew shouts. Busy telling stories, he did not see the doctor boarding. Do you think this is still the narrator's reaction, or is it already the author's, who, after the effort of this story, would also like to get out of here rather than work on the next one?

TO GO FURTHER

REFERENCE EDITION

CALVINO I., *Le Vicomte pourfendu*, Paris, Albin Michel, coll. «Le Livre de Poche», 1955 (reissued 2010).

BENCHMARK STUDIES

COLLECTIVE, «Italo Calvino», in *Encyclopædia Universalis*, Paris, 1980.

FUSCO M., «Un arbre généalogique?», in *Europe*, n° 815, March 1997.

«Les récits initiatiques», in *cndp.fr*, accessed on 22 August 2017. http://www.cndp.fr/crdp-creteil/telemaque/com-ite/initiatique.htm

MILLET G. and LABBÉ D., *Le fantastique*, Paris, Belin, coll. «Sujets», 2005.

TODOROV T., *Introduction à la littérature fantastique*, Paris, Seuil, 1970.

Your opinion is important to us!
Leave a comment on the website of your online bookshop
and share your favourites on social networks!

Ebook EAN: 9782808686617
Paperback EAN: 9782808698016
Legal Deposit: D/2023/12603/1081

Cover: © Primento
Digital conception by Primento, the digital partner of publishers.

9 782808 698016